STAR WARS

RETURN OF THE JEDI

The Ewoks Join the Fight

By Bonnie Bogart

Illustrated by Diane de Groat

Random House 🏠 New York

Copyright © 1983 Lucasfilm Ltd. (LFL). All rights reserved under International and Pan-American Copyright Conventions. Published in the United States by Random House, Inc., New York, and simultaneously in Canada by Random House of Canada Limited, Toronto.
Library of Congress Cataloging in Publication Data: Bogart, Bonnie. The Ewoks join the fight. SUMMARY: The Ewoks, natives of a tiny moon called Endor, come to the aid of the Rebel Alliance in its climactic battle against the evil Galactic Empire. [1. Science fiction. 2. Outer space—Fiction] I. De Groat, Diane, ill. II. Title. PZ7.B635785Ew 1983 [E] 82-62384 ISBN: 0-394-85858-1 (trade); 0-394-95858-6 (lib. bdg.)
Manufactured in the United States of America   1 2 3 4 5 6 7 8 9 0
TM—Trademarks of LFL used by Random House, Inc., under authorization.

Long ago, in a galaxy far away, a brave band of Rebels was preparing to do battle with the mighty forces of the evil Empire. The Rebels were led by three good friends—Luke Skywalker, Princess Leia Organa, and Han Solo.

The Rebel plan was to blow up the Empire's new battle station, Death Star 2. But it wouldn't be easy. Death Star 2 was protected by an invisible energy shield. Nothing could pass through the shield unless the Emperor or his powerful commander, Darth Vader, allowed it.

The Rebels knew that the main controls for the shield were on a tiny, densely wooded moon called Endor. They would have to overpower—or outsmart—the Empire's Imperial troops to destroy the shield.

It was a very dangerous mission, so Han, Leia, and Luke rounded up their best fighters—the Wookiee Chewbacca and the two droids Artoo-Detoo and See-Threepio.

Soon they were ready.

As soon as the Rebels landed on Endor they set out into the dark forest of giant trees to look for the shield control bunker. But before they got very far, they spotted two Imperial scouts in a clearing. The scouts' speeder bikes were parked nearby.

"I'll handle this," said Han Solo. And before anyone could stop him, he attacked the scouts.

"Uh-oh," said Leia. "Here come three more scouts. We'd better stop them or they'll warn the Imperial troops at the shield bunker."

"Right," said Luke. "You take that one, and I'll take those two." He grabbed one of the scouts' speeder bikes. Leia jumped on the other—and they were off!

Leia zoomed through the forest. She had almost caught up to the scout when he pulled out a laser gun and fired at her bike.

VAROOM! Leia's bike exploded and she went flying into a thicket. She landed so hard that she was knocked out.

When she came to, a strange little furry creature with big brown eyes was staring down at her.

"Who are you?" asked the Princess, sitting up with a groan. The creature, an Ewok named Wicket, backed away nervously when Leia spoke. Then he circled her suspiciously, poking at her with his wooden spear.

"Hey! Cut it out!" said Leia. "I won't hurt you—I promise."

Suddenly there was a rustling in the bushes—an Imperial scout! Wicket disappeared behind a log and Leia ducked, just missing a laser bolt.

Before she could get away, the scout grabbed her.

Without warning, a furry little hand came out of the bushes and jabbed the scout in the leg with a spear. The scout jumped in surprise and pain, and Leia quickly knocked him out.

She turned to her furry new friend. "Come on! Let's get out of here!"

Wicket seemed to understand. Squeaking excitedly, he tugged at Leia's sleeve and led her into the forest.

Meanwhile, Luke, Han, Chewie, and the two droids moved quietly through the trees. They had beaten the Imperial scouts and now they were looking for Leia. Suddenly Artoo beeped. He had found Leia's wrecked speeder bike.

"Oh, dear," said Threepio. "It appears that she ran into trouble."

"Brilliant observation," said Han. "But where is she now?"

Chewie sniffed the air. Then he barked and took off into the trees. The others followed him into a clearing. He was staring at a tall stake planted in the ground. There were pieces of meat hanging on it.

Chewie couldn't resist—he reached for a piece of meat.

"Wait! Don't!" warned Luke. But it was too late. SPROINGG! A trap went off and the entire group was caught in an Ewok net!

Artoo beeped wildly and Chewie howled with regret.

"Calm down, everyone," said Luke. "Artoo, can you cut us out of this thing?"

Artoo extended his cutting arm and got to work. He sliced up the net, and everyone tumbled to the ground.

When they got to their feet, they were surrounded—by a group of Ewoks with spears! The little creatures squeaked and chattered at the Rebels.

"Threepio," said Luke, "can you understand them?"

The golden droid could speak six million languages. When he talked to the Ewoks in their own language, they dropped their spears and bowed down to him.

Threepio was amazed. "They think I'm some sort of god!" he told his friends. They all laughed. But they stopped laughing when the Ewoks tied them up roughly and carried them through the forest.

Only Threepio was not taken prisoner. He was carried through the forest on a litter made of branches, like a king!

At last the procession arrived at the Ewok village. The Ewok chief, Chirpa, and the tribal medicine man, Logray, came out of a big hut. With them was Princess Leia.

When she saw the Rebels, Leia cried, "Threepio! Tell them these are my friends! They must be freed!"

Threepio spoke to Chirpa and Logray, but they would not set the Rebels free. The Ewoks did not trust humans.

"Threepio," said Luke quietly, "tell them to let us go or you'll get angry and use your magic."

Threepio was puzzled. He relayed the message and then asked, "What magic, Master Luke?"

Luke didn't answer. Instead he closed his eyes and concentrated . . . on the Force. He used his powers as a Jedi Knight to raise Threepio high into the air. Then he spun the droid around, faster and faster, like a bright golden top.

The Ewoks chattered and squeaked. Now they believed that Threepio was a very powerful god indeed! They untied the Rebel prisoners right away, and Leia embraced her friends.

That night the Rebels and the Ewoks sat together in Chief Chirpa's firelit hut. Threepio told the Ewoks about the war between the brave Rebel Alliance and the evil Empire.

When the Ewoks understood that the Imperial scouts on their tiny moon were part of a vast, deadly army, they talked among themselves for a long time. Then Chief Chirpa stood and spoke to them all. When he finished, the Ewoks cheered and beat their drums.

"The Chief has vowed to help us rid their land of the evil ones," Threepio told the Rebels. "His scouts will show us the fastest way to the shield control bunker!"

As the Rebels and the Ewoks prepared for their mission, Luke took Leia aside.

"Leia, I must go . . . I must try to save Darth Vader. He is my father."

"But, Luke . . . !" cried Leia.

"There is good in him. There must be. I have to try."

Luke and Leia embraced. "Be careful," she said. And Luke quickly followed the path out of the village.

The next day the Rebel strike squad stood on a ridge overlooking the shield control bunker. With them were several Ewoks, including their guides, Paploo and Teebo.

Guarding the bunker were three heavily armed Imperial scouts.

Suddenly the Rebels heard shouting from below. Paploo had crept down and stolen one of the scouts' speeder bikes! He roared off into the forest, and two of the three scouts chased after him.

"Not bad for a little ball of fuzz," commented Han. Then he and the squad quickly overpowered the last guard and broke into the shield bunker.

The Rebels raced to the control room and began to set their explosive charges.

"Hurry, Han," said Leia, who was watching the screen on the control panel. "We've got to destroy the shield right away! The Rebel fleet is being attacked!"

All at once the door flew open and a dozen Imperial scouts burst in. They overpowered the Rebels and led them out of the bunker.

The situation looked hopeless.

Teebo was watching the bunker from a tree. When the scouts and their prisoners appeared, he sounded the Ewok attack call. And at his signal hundreds of Ewoks came to the aid of the Rebels. They dropped from the trees and came swinging into the clearing on vines.

Ewoks swooped down in handmade hang gliders,
attacking the scouts with clubs and hatchets.

They fired a boulder
from a catapult in the forest,
knocking down an Imperial
walker.

They hurled sharp rocks at the scouts and shot at them with arrows.

Up on a ridge, they chopped at vines to release huge logs that came crashing down to smash another Imperial walker.

In the confusion Han and Leia broke away and ran back into the bunker.

They raced to the control room and set their charges with lightning speed. They ignited them and ran out of the bunker.

Seconds later the bunker exploded with a tremendous BOOM! The invisible energy shield was destroyed! Now the Rebel fleet could fly into the Death Star—and blow it up!

Before long the Rebels and their Ewok friends saw a gigantic explosion in space. They had won! The Death Star—and its evil rulers—were gone forever!

That night the Ewoks danced around a bonfire in their village square. The sound of their victorious drumbeats rang out into the night.

Han, Leia, and Chewie kept watch near the path. Suddenly Artoo began to beep joyfully. Luke walked into the village. He was safe!

"The Emperor is dead," Luke told his friends. "And Darth Vader. . . he is dead too."

Leia took Luke's hand. "You tried to save him," she whispered.

"I tried," said Luke sadly. "But it was too late for him."

Luke's friends embraced him. Then they turned back to the village to celebrate the victory they had all won together.